Gargoylz

Get Up To Mischief

Gargoylz: grotesque stone creatures found on old buildings, spouting rainwater from the guttering. Sometimes seen causing mischief and mayhem before scampering away over rooftops.

Peter

Read all the
Gargoylz adventures!

Gargoylz on the Loose!

Gargoylz Get Up to Mischief

Gargoylz at a Midnight Feast

Gargoylz Take a Trip

Gargoylz

Get Up To Mischief

Burchett & Vogler

illustrated by Leighton Noyes

RED FOX

GARGOYLZ GET UP TO MISCHIEF
A RED FOX BOOK 978 1 862 30836 7

First published in Great Britain by Red Fox,
an imprint of Random House Children's Books
A Random House Group Company

This edition published 2009

1 3 5 7 9 10 8 6 4 2

Series created and developed by Amber Caravéo
Copyright © Random House Children's Books, 2009

The Random House Group Limited supports the Forest Stewardship
Council (FSC), the leading international forest certification organization.
All our titles that are printed on Greenpeace-approved FSC-certified paper
carry the FSC logo. Our paper procurement policy can be found at
www.rbooks.co.uk/environment

Set in Bembo Schoolbook

Red Fox Books are published by Random House Children's Books,
61–63 Uxbridge Road, London W5 5SA

www.**kids**at**randomhouse**.co.uk
www.**rbooks**.co.uk

Addresses for companies within The Random House Group Limited can be
found at: www.randomhouse.co.uk/offices.htm

THE RANDOM HOUSE GROUP Limited Reg. No. 954009

A CIP catalogue record for this book is available from the British Library.

Printed in the UK by CPI Bookmarque, Croydon CR0 4TD

For Elizabeth Vogler, who must remember that although Gargoylz are allowed to climb buildings, she is not!

– Burchett & Vogler

For my nephew smElliot, who's a bit like Max

– Leighton Noyes

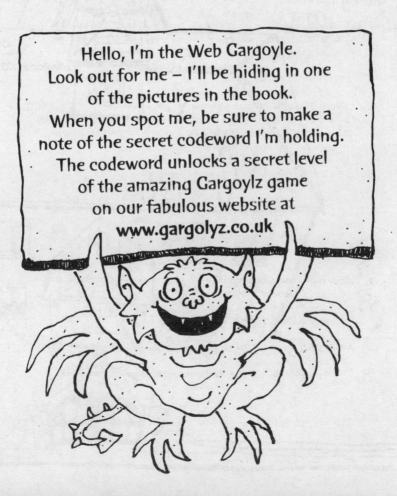

Hello, I'm the Web Gargoyle.
Look out for me – I'll be hiding in one
of the pictures in the book.
When you spot me, be sure to make a
note of the secret codeword I'm holding.
The codeword unlocks a secret level
of the amazing Gargoylz game
on our fabulous website at
www.gargolyz.co.uk

Oldacre Primary School

little frog
looking for
yummy flies

garden

staff
car park

staffroom

playing field

playground

St Mark's Church

playground

School Report - Max Black

Days absent: 0

Days late: 0

Max is a bright boy. If he spent as much time on his school work as he does on annoying Lucinda Tellingly he would get much better marks. I am pleased to see that he enjoys exercise - although I do not count running down corridors making racing car noises. Also I would be glad if he did not shout "Awesome" quite so loudly every time we have football practice.

Class teacher - Miss Deirdre Bleet

The only good thing I can say about Max Black is that he is always early for school. However, he is the last one into the classroom. He spends far too much time playing tricks with Ben Neal. Mrs Pumpkin is still off sick after discovering an earwig farm in her handbag. Max ignores all school rules. He has recently developed a curious interest in drainpipes and has been seen talking to the wall. This behaviour is outrageous and must stop.

Head teacher - Hagatha Hogsbottom (Mrs)

School Report - Ben Neal

Days absent: 0

Days late: 0

Ben has many abilities which he does not always use. He works very hard at dreaming up tricks to play, which gives him very little time to concentrate on his learning. He enjoys football and skateboarding - indeed, he and his board can frequently be found upside down in a flowerbed.

Class teacher - Miss Deirdre Bleet

Ben Neal is a strange boy. He is often to be found grinning at gutters.

He constantly breaks school rule number 742: boys must not break school rules.

Ben thinks he can get away with anything by flashing his blue eyes and looking innocent. I am not fooled.

Indeed I am still waiting for him and Max Black to write a note of apology to Mr Bucket the caretaker. Gluing his wellington boots to the staffroom ceiling was outrageous!

Head teacher - Hagatha Hogsbottom (Mrs)

Contents

1. Gnome, Sweet Gnome   1

2. Kitten Caper   27

3. Toby Stows Away   61

4. Science and Snakes   89

1. Gnome, Sweet Gnome

It was Saturday morning. Nine-year-old Max Black zoomed along in his imaginary spy car and screeched to a halt outside Oldacre Primary School. His best friend Ben was waiting for him.

"I can't believe we're at school at the weekend!" said Max.

"Neither can I." Ben grinned at him. "But at least we're not going in."

"You're right," said Max. "Ready for our new mission, Agent Neal?"

"Of course," said Ben. "Secret Plan: Take the Gargoylz to Your Nan's. But where are

Toby and Zack? They said they'd meet us here. We can't go without them."

"Greetingz!" came a growly purr from the graveyard and a small creature flew up onto the churchyard wall.

Max activated his spy radar to check him out: monkey face, pointy ears, stony skin. He knew what that meant. It was Toby, their gargoyle friend.

Max and Ben had a big secret. The gargoylz that hung on the ancient church next to their school were not the stone statues that everyone thought they were.

They were alive. And they'd made friends with Max and Ben. Like the boys, the gargoylz enjoyed having fun and playing tricks. It was a perfect partnership!

Toby wagged his pointy tail at the boys. "Ready for bramble collecting?" he asked as he fluttered his leafy wings and flew over to perch on Max's shoulder. All gargoylz had a special power and Toby's was flying. Although lots of the gargoylz had wings, Toby was the only one the boys had met who could use them to actually fly.

This weekend Toby and Zack were on bramble-collecting duty for all the other gargoylz. Prickly plants were their favourite food, and Max knew exactly where they could get plenty of those – his nan's garden.

"We brought our rucksacks so that you can hide inside them," said Max. "You mustn't be seen trotting along the high street."

"Quite right!" declared Toby. He flew into Ben's bag and popped his head out of the top. "Well, what are we waiting for? I want to get my pawz on those thorny snacks."

"And I want to get my hands on Nan's cupcakes," said Max. "Best things in the world."

"We can't go without Zack," said Ben, looking around. "Where is he?"

"Bramblz, thistlz, anything with pricklz!" came a cheeky voice beside him.

4

There was no one to be seen.

"Invisible again, Zack?" Max laughed.

POP! A gargoyle with a fuzzy mane and a tuft on his head appeared on the wall. He zipped up and down and then sat there panting, his tongue hanging out. "No bag for me," he declared, looking at Max's open rucksack. "I'll disappear instead. My special gargoyle power. Won't be seen."

"Yes you will," said Ben. "You're always appearing when you don't mean to."

"Good point," chortled Zack.

He hopped into Max's rucksack. "Come on. I'm hungry."

"Hold on tight," yelled Max, zooming off at top speed. "We're using our spy car and it's really fast."

Two minutes later they were knocking on a bright blue door. It opened. Max checked his spy radar: curly hair, big smile, apron covered in flour. It was Nan, codename: Supercook.

"Hello, dears." She beamed as the boys followed her towards the kitchen. "You're just in time. I've been baking."

Ben's rucksack gave a shake.

"Spluttering gutterz!" came a growly voice from inside. "Smellz delicious."

"Glad you think so, Ben," replied Nan as they followed her into the kitchen. "But what's happened to your voice? It sounds as if you've got a cold. I'll give you some of my special cure later."

"Thanks, Mrs Black," said Ben politely, nudging his rucksack with his elbow to keep Toby quiet.

Max made a face at his friend. Nan might be the best cupcake maker in the world but her homemade medicines were foul.

Nan opened the back door. "Now why don't you go and play in the garden like

you usually do, and I'll bring some freshly baked cupcakes out in a little while."

The boys grinned and raced across the lawn to the bottom of the garden where Nan's blackberry bushes grew in a weedy tangle. They were hidden from the rest of the garden by an apple tree and some rhododendrons. Max and Ben opened their rucksacks and let the gargoylz out.

"What a feast!" gasped Toby, his eyes

on stalks at the sight of the brambles and
nettles.

"Let me at 'em!" cried Zack, diving
straight into the thorns.

"Wait for me," called Toby, flapping his
wings and zooming in after him.

"We'll help you pick them," said Max.
"I've got top secret spy gloves." He pulled
them out of his rucksack. "They're my
dad's best ones. I had to sneak them out.

They're brand new so they're sure to be prickle-proof."

"And I've got special agent bramble slicers," said Ben, waving a pair of scissors. "They're my sister's. She uses them for her scrapbook. She'd explode if she knew I had them. You hold the brambles and I'll cut them."

Max and Ben soon had a big pile of bramble stalks by their feet. Suddenly it began to heave and wobble as if it was alive. Then Toby's head popped out, scattering branches and leaves everywhere.

"Tasty bramblz," he said, with his mouth full. "You two are wonderful collectors."

Max laughed. "How many have you collected? Don't forget you two are supposed to be picking them for all the

other gargoylz as well. You're not meant to eat them all."

Toby looked sheepish. "But they're so delicious."

POP! A dragony tail appeared beside him followed by the rest of Zack. "Best place for pricklz ever," he said, munching away.

"Coo-ee, boys!"

"Hide!" whispered Max. "It's Nan. She mustn't see you."

ZOOM! ZOOM! Zack and Toby jumped out of the bramble pile and dived headfirst into the bushes just as Nan

appeared with a tray. She set it down on
the grass.

"I've brought you some juice and
cupcakes. I wasn't sure which toppings
you'd like so there's a selection."

"Thanks, Nan," said Max, eyeing the
huge pile of brightly coloured iced cakes in
delight.

There was a rustling in the bushes
followed by a licking of stone lips, and a
pair of stone ears suddenly popped up.

Nan frowned. "I hope that's not a cat in my blackberries," she muttered.

"A cat?" came Toby's indignant growl from the bush.

"Ben dear," said Nan. "Your voice is getting worse. I'm going straight back in to make some of my special cold cure."

She suddenly noticed the pile of brambles. "What do you want those for?" she asked.

"Er . . . they're for the school rabbit," said Max quickly.

"Yes . . . he's staying at my house for the weekend," added Ben.

Nan looked puzzled. "They're a bit prickly for a rabbit, aren't they?"

"It's . . . it's . . . a very rare rabbit," said

Max. "Isn't it, Ben?"

"Yes. It's a . . . er . . . Bramble-eating
Stony Church Rabbit," gabbled Ben. "It
loves prickly things."

"Well, fancy that." Nan turned to go
back into the house. "Enjoy your cakes."

As soon as she'd gone the gargoylz
scampered out.

"Cat indeed!" exclaimed Toby.
"Ferocious yowling creatures with
too much fur—" He suddenly saw the
cupcakes. "Are these like the cookiez I
had at school?" he asked eagerly. "I love
cookiez."

"They're the cupcakes I told you

about," said Max, holding out the plate. "Try one."

Toby stretched out a paw and grabbed a cake, then stuffed it in his mouth. "Dangling drainpipes, they're delicious!" he sighed happily.

"Let me try! Let me try!" Zack cried, gobbling up a cake and grabbing two more – one in each paw. He darted off, sat down in the weeds and munched noisily.

Three minutes later every cake had gone. Both gargoylz lay on the grass, bellies bulging.

"Shame there aren't any more," said Toby.

"You've had ten!" Max exclaimed.

"Ben and I were lucky to get any once you two started!"

"Coo-ee," came Nan's voice. "I've brought a bag for the brambles – and my special cold cure for you, Ben."

POP! Zack vanished. Toby struggled to his feet but he didn't have time to hide. He was stranded on the grass in full view. He froze, a horrified expression on his face, as Nan appeared holding out a mug of bubbling green liquid. It smelled like old socks.

She spotted Toby immediately. "What a lovely little garden gnome!" she said, putting the mug down on the grass and giving him a poke. "Did you make him at school, Max?"

"No ... er ... yes," said Max. How was

he going to get Toby out of this?

"Look at his diddy little hands and his little round tummy," Nan went on. "He'd look lovely in my rockery."

"I can't let you keep him, Nan," said Max hurriedly. "He's got to go back to the chur— I mean, school. He's not finished."

"I can see that now," said his grandmother kindly. "His face looks ever so ugly."

There was a growly snort of laughter in the air behind them from Zack.

Nan looked anxiously at Ben. "You still don't sound right, dear," she said. "Drink up your medicine like a good boy."

"Er . . ." quavered Ben, bending down to pick up the revolting drink.

Max could see his friend needed a

plan – Operation Spill the Drink. But before he could do anything there was a faint slurping noise from the mug. The boys gazed down in astonishment as the bubbling green liquid quickly disappeared. Max hid a grin. Invisible Zack must have sneaked out of the bushes. Luckily Nan didn't seem to have noticed.

Ben swept up the empty mug and pretended to drink the mixture down in one gulp. "Thanks." He grinned. "It was . . . tasty."

An almighty gargoyle burp filled the air. "Pardon me!" said Ben quickly.

"My cure never fails," chirped Nan. "See, your voice is back to normal already." She bent down and patted Toby on the head. "And I've got the very thing for you, Mr Gnome. I'll be back in a jiffy."

She bustled off to the house. Max and Ben burst out laughing.

POP! Zack appeared, wiping green goo off his chin. "Sorry, Ben. Drank it all. Couldn't resist. Nearly as tasty as bramblz." He raced over to Toby. "Mr Gnome!" he giggled, skipping around him. "Mr Gnome!"

Toby looked furious. "Mr Gnome!" he spluttered, jumping to his feet. "I'm an ancient stone gargoyle who's lived proudly on the church for more than eight hundred

yearz and your nan thinks I'm a garden
ornament!"

"Ugly garden ornament!" chuckled
Zack, rolling on his back and kicking his
legs in the air.

"Coo-ee!" Nan was suddenly back,
waving something small and red.

POP! Zack disappeared. Toby froze
again.

"All garden gnomes should have one of
these," she said.

Max and Ben tried desperately not to

laugh as Nan carefully
fitted a pointy, red
woolly hat over Toby's
monkey ears.

"How sweet!"
She beamed,
tickling him
under the chin.
"Who's a smart
Mr Gnome then?"

Max suddenly realized he could see a tail appearing on the grass in front of him . . . then a paw . . . then an ear . . . Zack was forgetting to stay invisible. Max stepped smartly in front of him but it was too late.

"What's that behind you, dear?" asked Nan, peering round him. Zack was completely visible now. "Oh, you didn't tell me there was a little girly one as well!" she exclaimed. "Did you make her, Ben? She's so sweet!" Nan patted Zack's fuzzy stone mane. "You've even tried to give her some hair." She reached into her apron pocket and pulled out a lacy handkerchief. "I haven't got another hat," she explained, "but this will do nicely." She fixed the hankie round Zack's head like a scarf and tied it under his chin. "Mr and Mrs Gnome. What a lovely couple!"

"Thanks, Nan," gulped Max. He had to get away before he burst out laughing. "We have to be off now. Back to Ben's house. To give the rabbit its lunch."

"Yes, you get along and give that Stony Church thingamabob a real treat," agreed Nan, helping the boys to put the brambles into the bag. While her back was turned Max beckoned to the gargoylz. They hopped into the rucksacks.

"I'll see you soon," Nan called, waving the boys off from the garden gate.

SECRET CODEWORD:
PLOT

Max and Ben reached the church wall and opened their bags. The gargoylz tumbled out and Max handed Toby the bag of brambles.

"Let's go home, Mr Gnome!" Zack laughed.

"All right, Mrs Gnome," answered Toby. "Little girly one!"

"Hmph!" snorted Zack. "Make a pact. No more gnome talk."

"Agreed," said Toby as they scampered off and the boys headed home. "But it was funny when she called you a girl. I haven't laughed so much since I put nettlz in the vicar's breakfast."

2. Kitten Caper

Secret Agent Max Black strolled along the road on his way to school. He heard the sound of wheels racing over the pavement and turned on his spy radar: blond hair, blue eyes, battered knee pads. It was Agent Ben Neal, riding a gleaming new skateboard.

"Awesome!" Max exclaimed as Ben stopped and flipped the shiny red board into his hand. "That's the Speed King!"

"It's new," said Ben proudly. "I've brought it to show everyone this afternoon when all the Year Four classes get together to do Hobbies Talk."

They ran through the school gates.

"Greetingz!"

The monkey face of a cheeky gargoyle was hanging down from the school roof.

Max beamed. "Hello there, Toby." Then he spotted something on the roof behind him. Something small and fluffy. "There's a kitten stuck up there!" he gasped, pointing.

"Poor thing," said Ben. "Can you rescue it, Toby?"

To their surprise Toby burst out laughing. "Spluttering gutterz!" he guffawed. "That's not a kitten. That's my gargoyle friend Theophilus. His special power is meant to be turning into a ferocious tiger but it never works. Theo, say hello to Max and Ben."

As they watched, the tabby ball of fluff gave a determined **miaow**. After a lot of wriggling it slowly changed shape until a gargoyle sat in its place. The new gargoyle had a long, tigerish tail and his golden stone was slightly stripy. His face was a bit like a cat's, with bristling whiskers and small, friendly-looking fangs. He stared at Max and Ben.

"Humanz!" he gasped with an anxious swish of his tail. "Help! They mustn't see us."

"It's OK, Theo." Toby laughed. "These two are my friends. They'll keep our secret."

"That's all right then." Theo beamed at Max and Ben. "Sorry if I frightened you when I was a ferocious tiger."

"You weren't exactly ferocious . . ." began Max.

"Wasn't I?" said Theo.

"And you weren't exactly a tiger," Ben told him.

"Wasn't I?" sighed Theo.

"More of a kitten really," explained Max with an apologetic grin.

"Oh dear," said Theo dejectedly. "I was so sure I'd become a tiger this time. The thing is, I'm only four hundred and twelve years old. I haven't had long to practise."

"You were a very good kitten," Max reassured him.

"Keep practising and you'll be the most ferocious tiger in the world," said Toby. "It'll only take another hundred years or so." He caught sight of the Speed King. "What's that?"

"It's my new skateboard," said Ben, holding it up for him to see.

"New board?" came a harsh voice behind them. Toby and Theo froze into statues.

Max's spy radar picked up trouble: shaved head, big fists, sticky-out ears. He knew what that meant.

It was Enemy Agent Barry Price, also known as The Basher, codename: School Bully.

The next minute The Basher had Ben's skateboard in his hands.

"Give it back, Barry!" Ben pleaded. "You can have a look at it this afternoon when our classes get together."

"No one'll want to see this rubbish," scoffed The Basher. "Not when I show them what I've brought." He tapped his school bag with a gloating grin.

"What *have* you brought then?" asked Max.

"It's a secret," Barry said, and, to their horror, jumped on Ben's skateboard. "See you later!"

He streaked off across the playground, whooping triumphantly and bashing kids over as he went.

Suddenly Max saw a tall figure emerging
from the school door. Grey hair, beaky
nose, face like thunder. He
knew what that meant. It was
Enemy Agent Mrs Hogsbottom,
commonly known as Mrs Hogsbum,
codename: Stinky Head Teacher.
The Basher zoomed past the door and
went **smack!** straight into her, knocking
her right off her feet.

"Outrageous!" shrieked Mrs
Hogsbottom, staggering up
again and staring at
Barry with her laser
vision. "School rule
number twenty-
seven. The head
teacher must
not be run
over without
permission. I
shall keep this

36

monstrosity until home time."

"I never thought I'd say this," gasped Max, "but Mrs Hogsbum's done us a favour. She's taken the Speed King off The Basher for us."

"I'll go and get it back," said Ben eagerly.

The boys rushed over to the furious head teacher, who was brushing gravel off her bony knees. The Basher stood smirking behind her.

"What do you two want?" she snapped as soon as she saw them.

"The skateboard's mine, Mrs Hogsbottom," Ben began to explain. "Could I have it back please?"

"Certainly not!" sniffed the head teacher. "If you hadn't

lent it to Barry Price this wouldn't have happened."

"I didn't lend it," said Ben. "He snatched it." He put on his wide-eyed, pleading look. It always worked on the dinner ladies, who gave him extra pudding. It never worked on Mrs Hogsbottom.

"No excuses," she snapped, picking up the Speed King and tucking it firmly under her arm.

"But Ben has to show it to everyone in

class later," pleaded Max. "He brought it in specially for the talk."

"Ben should have thought of that when he lent it to Barry Price," said Mrs Hogsbottom crossly. "He can have it back after school." She turned on her heel and marched towards the door.

The Basher poked his face into Ben's.

"What a shame!" he sniggered.

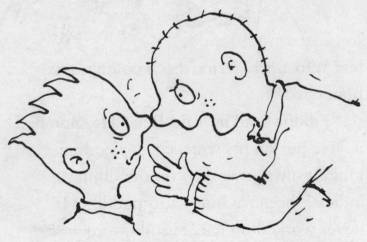

"Still, never mind. No one would have listened to you whingeing on about skateboarding. My hobby's much better."

He strutted off, pushing a couple of

small footballers out of the way as he went.

"I don't reckon he's got anything better than your Speed King," said Max when The Basher was out of earshot.

"At least he's got *something*," sighed Ben miserably.

"That was really mean," came a growly purr. Toby was watching The Basher go. "Wish I had my catapult with me. I'd fire some acorns at him."

"When he comes back I'm going to turn into a tiger," said Theo. He stretched out a front paw. Three tiny claws appeared. "That'll give him a scare."

The bell rang. Mrs Hogsbottom stood by the door, fuming.

"We'd better go in," sighed Max, "before she explodes."

"That was the worst morning in the history of worst mornings," said Ben at lunch time. "We haven't played a trick on anyone."

"We've been too busy thinking about how to get our own back on The Basher," Max pointed out.

"And my poor Speed King is being held prisoner," said Ben. "Mrs Hogsbum is probably feeding it to her crocodiles right now."

Max's eyes suddenly lit up. "Don't despair, Agent Neal," he said. "We'll do a great trick and get our own back at the same time." He leaned forward to whisper in Ben's ear, "Barry's got something in his bag that he reckons is really cool, right?"

Ben nodded. "Right, Agent Black."

"Then our mission is to swap it for something stupid and girly." Max grinned. "When he gets it out to show everyone he'll be dead embarrassed."

"Good plan!" breathed Ben. "And I know just the thing – my sister Arabella's ballet tutu. It's all pink and frilly and horrible. It's in her ballet bag. Only one problem," he added with a frown. "The bag is in the girls' cloakroom and boys are not allowed in there. If we get caught we'll never hear the end of it."

"I know someone who can help us with that!" said Max, nodding up at the roof.

"Toby!" exclaimed Ben as their
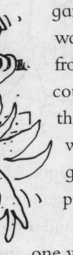
gargoyle friend waved at them from a gutter. "He could fly in through the cloakroom window and get it for us, no problem."

Making sure no one was looking, the boys sauntered over towards Toby.

"Greetingz!" called Toby chirpily.

"Hi, Toby," Max called back. "Want to help with a trick?"

Toby's yellow eyes lit up and his dragon tail swished. "A trick?" he said eagerly. "A prank? Dangling drainpipes! Tell me all about it!"

Max gave Toby his instructions for Secret Plan: Tutu. Chuckling, the little gargoyle zoomed off to the girls' cloakroom window. In a flash he was back with Arabella's pink tutu in his paws.

"I can hardly bear to touch it, it's so girly," declared Max, pulling a disgusted face. "It's lucky all the school rucksacks look the same. We'll swap my bag for Barry's." He stuffed the tutu in his bag.

"There's one thing we haven't thought of," said Ben. "How are we going to stop The Basher seeing when we swap them round? It's not much of a trick if he catches us at it!"

"Can I join in?" Theo's stripy head popped up over the gutter. "Maybe I'll manage a tiger this time."

"No, we need a kitten," cried Ben, "for Secret Plan: Kitten Diversion. Agent Black, do you remember when that big black cat jumped through the window of our classroom last term? Everyone went all gooey and Miss Bleet forgot to give us any maths homework. Think what would happen if a sweet little tabby kitten came in instead. No one would see us making the bag switch then."

"I like your thinking, Agent Neal," said Max. "Listen, Theo, we've got a trick to play this afternoon and we need everyone to be looking at you while we're setting it up."

A broad grin spread over Theo's whiskery face. "What do I have to do?" he asked, almost falling off the roof in excitement.

"We need you to come in through our classroom window this afternoon," said Max. "While everyone's looking at you, we'll swap The Basher's bag with the one that has the frilly pink tutu in it. All the class will laugh when he gets it out."

"Serve the bully right," said Toby.

"I can do that!" cried Theo.

Just then the bell rang.

"Right!" said Max. "I'll leave a window open for you this afternoon. Come in as soon as we start the lesson. When we've swapped the bags, I'll say the password and you can skedaddle."

"Yes, sir!" Theo sat up proudly. "What's the password?"

"Tiddles," said Max.

Straight after register it was time for Hobbies Talk. The other class in their year group came in, led by Barry.

"Shove up!" he said nastily, pushing a row of girls out of the way.

"Quick," Max whispered to Ben. "Go and grab us a couple of seats behind The Basher. I'll open a window. I hope Theo remembers what to do."

Max joined Ben in the row behind the bully. Barry turned and smirked at the boys.

"I'm looking forward to your talk, Ben," he sneered. "What's it about? Oh yes, I remember. Nothing!"

"Quiet please," came a quavery voice.

Max's spy radar snapped into action:

short and dumpy, limp brown hair, silly half-moon glasses. It was Enemy Agent Miss Bleet, codename: Wimpy Teacher.

"Welcome to Hobbies Talk," Miss Bleet said feebly. "Lucinda, you start."

There was a groan as Lucinda Tellingly marched up to the front clutching her huge collection of plastic ponies.

"I hope Theo comes in soon," muttered Max. "I can't bear to hear much of this."

"These are my special horses," Lucinda began to coo. "They all have names and— Oooh, look at the darling kitten!"

Everyone turned to where she was pointing. Theo, in his cutest tabby form, was perched on the window ledge. He jumped into the room and darted about, as if he was chasing imaginary mice.

"Here, sweetums!" cooed Miss Bleet, bending down. Theo rubbed round her ankles and purred.

"Now's our chance," hissed Max. "All eyes are on Theo, even The Basher's!"

"Ready for synchronized bag switching?" asked Ben.

Max nodded. Ben reached under Barry's chair and snatched up the Basher's bag. Max put his own in its place. Then they both sat back and looked innocent.

"Tiddles!" Max called. Everyone stared at him in astonishment. "Er . . . I recognize the cat . . . He's called Tiddles and he lives down my road," Max explained with a shrug.

But Theo didn't take his cue and jump out of the window. He was having too much fun. He was now sitting on Miss Bleet's table, playing with her pencil.

"Tiddles!" said Max loudly.

Theo let go of the pencil but rolled over onto his back, looking adorable and knocking Miss Bleet's papers to the floor.

"We won't have time for the trick at this rate," Ben muttered to Max.

"TIDDLES!" yelled Max.

Theo scrambled to his feet and bolted out of the window with a loud **miaow**.

"How mean!" said Lucinda, glaring at Max. "Scaring the poor little thing like that."

"Quiet please," said Miss Bleet, in a fluster. "The cat's gone. Who'd like to go next?"

"But I haven't—" began Lucinda.

"Me!" interrupted Barry Price, grabbing the bag under his chair and marching to the front. "You won't want to listen to anyone else after my go. I've got the best hobby in the world!" He delved into his bag. "Every Saturday I wear this." He pulled out the pink tutu and held it up proudly.

For a long moment there was a shocked silence in the class and then everyone burst out laughing. The Basher suddenly realized what he was holding. He stared at the tutu as if it was a poisonous snake.

"This isn't mine!" he yelled, flinging it to the floor. "Where's my crash helmet? That's what I was going to show you. I do go-karting every weekend."

"You shouldn't be ashamed of enjoying ballet, Barry," said Miss Bleet kindly. "We'd all like to hear about it, wouldn't we, class?"

"YES!" The shout echoed around the
room.

"But I don't do ballet!" Barry made his
way back to his place, his face bright red.

"It's girly. I told you: I do go-karting."

Miss Bleet wasn't listening. "Now tell us all about why you choose to wear a tutu."

"I DON'T WEAR A STUPID TUTU!"

The Basher slumped down in his seat, glaring at everyone. He didn't say another word for the rest of the day. He didn't even notice when Max swapped the bags back.

As soon as the bell rang, Max and Ben dashed off to Mrs Hogsbottom's office to retrieve the Speed King.

"School Rule number four hundred and seventeen," she barked as soon as she saw them. "Boys must not dash into the head teacher's office to get their skateboards back. School rule two hundred and fifty-five . . ."

Five school rules later they were finally released. They ran to the school gate.

"Did you see The Basher's face when he realized what he was holding?" chuckled Ben. "Imagine him go-karting in a tutu!"

"Oh no! Your sister's tutu!" gasped Max. "It's still on the classroom floor!"

Ben turned white. "We're in big trouble. Come on, we've got to get it back without being seen."

They were just heading back towards the school door when something fell on

Ben's head. It was pink and frilly. Max looked up to see Toby on the school roof, with Theo next to him.

"That was a great trick you played on The Basher!" wheezed Toby as Ben struggled with the tutu on his head. "I haven't laughed so much since Theo chased a mouse up the vicar's trousers."

"Thanks, Toby." Max grinned. "And thanks, Theo — you were an awesome kitten."

"You wait till you see my tiger," said Theo. "Only another hundred years and I'll get it perfect."

Ben emerged from under the tutu. "If you go and put this back in Arabella's bag for me," he said, putting his skateboard on the ground, "I'll give you both a ride on my Speed King."

"Spluttering gutterz!" the gargoylz shouted together, grabbing the tutu and rushing off with it.

3. Toby Stows Away

Max and Ben jumped up from their seats. School was over for another day.

"I thought that maths lesson would never end," complained Max, grabbing his bag.

"It must have been about a hundred years long," agreed Ben. They made a dash for the classroom door.

"Freedom awaits!" yelled Max as they sped along the corridor and out into the playground. "And we've got important people to see."

"Important gargoylz!" Ben grinned.

They sprinted across to peer over the church wall.

"Hello," said a shy voice, and Barney's doggy face peeped round a gravestone. "Pleased to see you."

He began to waddle towards the boys when all of a sudden he jolted forward and rolled over and over. The spikes on his back stuck out, making him look like a hedgehog.

POP! Zach appeared out of thin air by his side, his fuzzy mane quivering around his face. "Sorry, Barney!" he cried.

"Bumped into you. Wasn't looking." **POP!**
He vanished again.

"Where's Toby?" asked Max.

"I don't know," said Barney, looking
around. "He was here a minute ago."

A window creaked open on the
other side of the playground.

"Outrageous!" came a
harsh voice.

Max spun round. It
was Mrs Hogsbottom.

"School rule
number three hundred
and eighty-two," she
screeched across the
playground. "Boys must
not talk to the wall! Get
yourselves home, NOW!"

"Yes, Mrs Hogsbottom," they called.

"We've got to go," Max hissed to
Barney. "See you tomorrow."

Barney gave them a cheery wave and

then crouched back down behind the gravestone. He put a paw to his lips. "Shhh!" he warned. "I'm going to jump out on Zack – if I'm fast enough."

Max and Ben set off home. "I hope Barney remembers not to make any of his special disgusting smells," said Ben. "Zack will know where he is at once."

Max hoisted his school bag onto his shoulders. "I wonder where Toby was."

"Probably playing a trick on the vicar," said Ben. "Come on, Agent Black, all aboard our Secret Agent Speedboat."

They zoomed off home.

Max burst through his back door into the kitchen and dropped his bag on the floor. There was someone at the table. He

activated his spy
radar: dark brown
hair, red jumper,
potato peeler in
hand. It was Mrs
Joanne Black,
codename: Mum.

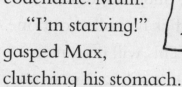

"I'm starving!"
gasped Max,
clutching his stomach.
He grabbed a packet of biscuits, ran into
the hall and made for the stairs. "Can I
have one?" he yelled over his shoulder.

"You can have one and one only,"
called Mum. "I don't want you spoiling
your dinner. And don't leave your bag
down here for me to fall over. Come back
and take it up to your bedroom."

Max had reached the top of the stairs.
He looked at the packet of biscuits and
sighed. He'd have to get his school bag
or his mother would keep on nagging.

With a clever spin, he was back down in the kitchen before she could say tidy up. He swung his bag over his shoulder, raced upstairs and flung it on the bed.

Then he sat on the floor, ready to eat his biscuit.

"Mum just doesn't understand a boy's stomach," he groaned as he pulled out one chocolate digestive. "This will disappear into the empty void. I could eat the whole packet and still have room for dinner – except peas. There'd be no room for peas."

"Greetingz!" came a voice from his bag. "What are peas?"

Max whipped round. Something was clambering out of his bag. His spy radar homed in: monkey face, pointy ears, cheeky smile. It was Toby, codename: Gargoyle Friend.

"Toby!" Max exclaimed. "Awesome. We can play all evening."

"Is that a cookie?" asked the gargoyle,

scrambling over and sniffing the packet.

"Yes," said Max. "These are chocolate digestives. They're delicious. Try one."

He handed Toby the biscuits. Mum had said he could only have one. That didn't mean Toby couldn't have one as well.

Max finished his and dived under his bed. "I've got something to show you," he called. At last he reappeared, empty-handed, his hair standing even more on end than usual. "Well, I will have when I find it. It's my remote-control car. I thought it was under the bed but there are only spiders there." He rummaged in a box of action figures, then threw all the shoes

out of his wardrobe. He emptied a drawer
onto a mountain of socks and underpants.
"Got it!" he cried at last, holding out a
shiny sports car. "You can have first go.
You just switch it
on and—"

He gawped.
Toby's monkey
face was covered in
chocolate and the
empty biscuit packet
was scrunched up
in his paw. He was
smiling blissfully.

"You've eaten the lot!" Max gasped.
"Mum'll think it was me. I'm going to be
in big trouble."

Toby looked worried. "Sorry, Max,"
he said. "I couldn't help myself. You were
right. They're delicious."

Max jumped to his feet. "I've had a
brainwave!" he said. "I'll sneak the packet

downstairs and put it in the cupboard.
Hopefully, Mum will think my sister Jessica
has eaten them all! Stay here. It won't
take me long to carry out my new secret
mission."

Agent Max Black crept down the stairs
and along the hall. The television was on
and he could see Enemy Agents Mum and
Jessica watching it. They were no match
for a superspy like him. He sneaked past

unseen and opened the kitchen door, making sure that it didn't creak. Then he skidded across to the cupboard. He reached up to put the empty packet back on the shelf.

"Max!" His mum was right behind him. He hadn't heard her. She must be wearing her special Enemy Agent Stealth Slippers. "What are you doing?" She saw the empty packet in his hand. "Have you eaten all the biscuits?"

"No!" said Max truthfully. "I only had one like you said."

"And I suppose the fairies had the rest," sighed his mother. "You'd better eat all your dinner."

"I will!"

"I'm giving you extra peas," she went on. "Now go up to the bathroom and wash your hands before you eat."

Max escaped.

He wasn't going to bother to wash his

hands. They weren't that dirty. He'd only made one mud pie at lunch time. Instead he dashed up to see Toby again.

"I've got to have my dinner now," he told him. "You must stay here until I get back. And no more trouble!"

"I'll be good," said Toby, looking around the room. "Lots for me to do."

"Max!" shouted his mum. "Dinner's on the table."

Mum doled out the apple crumble and handed it round. Max poured custard over it and tucked in. It was his favourite pudding.

Plop! A large drop of water splashed into his bowl. Then another.

Dad leaped to his feet. "We've got a leak!" he cried, pointing up at the ceiling, where a damp patch was spreading.

"Did you forget to turn the tap off, Max?" demanded Mum.

Max shook his head, but he had a nasty feeling he might know who did . . .

"Don't worry," he yelled as he charged down the hall. "I'll see to it."

He took the stairs two at a time and flung the bathroom door open. His jaw dropped in horror. The basin taps were full on and the plug was in. A bubbly pink waterfall was pouring all over the floor.

Toby had discovered Jessica's bubble bath. Max squelched across the room and turned the taps off.

"Toby!" he hissed.

There was no answer and no sign of his gargoyle friend.

"What have you been doing?" cried Mum. Max turned round. Mum and Dad were standing behind him, looking in horror at the flood.

"I didn't do it!" exclaimed Max. "I didn't even wash my hands!"

"You always try to wriggle out of it," said Dad crossly as Mum threw towels down to soak up the water. "I've had enough of your pranks, Max. Go to your room. No more apple crumble and no TV tonight."

Max thought about it. He was sorry
not to be finishing his pudding but he had
a much more important mission: Find
Toby. Who knew what other mischief the
gargoyle was going to get up to?

He rushed into his bedroom. He
looked under his bed and
in his cupboard and
rummaged through the
pile of underpants. No
gargoylz.

"Time to find clues,
Agent Black," he said
to himself.

He went back to
the bathroom, tiptoeing
in case his parents heard. No Toby
there. But on the landing carpet he saw a
line of small bubbly pawprints. "Excellent,"
he muttered. "I have a lead." The prints
trailed across to Jessica's room. He leaned
over the banister and listened. His family

was still eating crumble.
The coast was clear.
He followed the prints.

"Greetingz!" An upside-
down monkey face flashed
backwards and forwards
in front of him. Toby was
swinging from Jessica's
frilly lampshade. Max
looked around in
dismay. Jessica's toy box had
been emptied, every drawer was open
and there was green playdough covered in
tooth marks all over the floor.

"Did you make this mess?" Max
demanded, zooming round
putting everything back to
rights. He couldn't believe
he was tidying his sister's
bedroom!

"I was looking for more
biscuits," Toby explained.

"But all I found was that horrible green stuff. **Bleurgh!** Tasted disgusting."

"Come back to my room before you get me into worse trouble." Max went to the door to make sure there was no one about.

"Dangling drainpipes!" said Toby as he flew along the landing. "I haven't had this much fun since I put sneezing powder in the vicar's hankie! Let's play a trick on your family."

"I wish we could," sighed Max. "But I'd end up with no pudding for a week. I'd never survive. You'll have to try and behave yourself till tomorrow."

Back in his bedroom, Max rummaged under his pillow and found his Game Boy. "I've got this really cool game," he told Toby. "It's called Attack of the Martian Mushrooms. I'll play it first to show you what to do and then you can have a go." He showed Toby the brightly flashing screen. "You can hold it in your paws, can't you?"

"Course I can," said Toby, squatting down to watch.

Max clicked some buttons and started the game. He escaped in a rocket before the mushrooms captured him. Then, with some amazing skill, he leaped to level sixty-two. "One more minute and you can have a go, Toby," he murmured as he concentrated on blasting the Monster Fungus that had him in its evil tendrils.

At last he had reached the Toadstool of Terror. "I'll just save my game and—" Max suddenly realized it had gone very quiet in his bedroom. He looked up. Toby was nowhere to be seen.

"Oh, no," he groaned, leaping to his feet. "Not again!"

He sped across the landing, checking every room. He peered inside the airing cupboard and pulled out all the clothes in the dirty washing basket, scattering them on the carpet.

No gargoyle in sight!

There was only one thing for it. Agent Black was going to have to venture into enemy territory. He would have to go downstairs and search there – and all without his parents seeing him.

"Activate invisibility shield," he muttered.

He crept down the stairs and checked the hall. The door to the cupboard under the stairs was open. He flashed past the lounge with an expert commando roll and stuck his head into the cupboard. It was a total mess. Shoes, cloths, polish — everything looked as if it had been picked up and tossed in the air.

Good, thought Max. *Toby's been here. I'm getting close.*

He shut the door so no one would notice the disaster area and moved stealthily on to the kitchen. He put his secret listening device — codename: Ear — to the door. He could hear a lot of splashing. He opened the door a crack — and gawped! Toby was sitting in the sink, playing with the pots and pans. The water was slopping over the edge and the room was filled with bubbles of washing-up liquid.

Max slid across the wet floor. He put his hands into the soapy water to grab his gargoyle friend. "Toby!" he gasped. "You've got to come—"

"What have you got there?"

Max's spy radar went into overdrive: small, shriekingly loud and a complete pest. He knew what that meant. It was Enemy Agent Jessica Black, codename: Disgusting Little Sister. She was pointing at Toby, who was sitting in a saucepan.

"It's nothing," Max said quickly, moving to stand in between his sister and the soapy gargoyle.

"You've got an animal there," she insisted, trying to push past him. "Let me see it."

"No, Jess," said Max through gritted teeth. "Go away!"

"Mum!" yelled Jessica.

"Be quiet," begged Max. "I'll give you anything you want, only don't get Mum in here."

"MUM!" Jessica stuck her tongue out at him and ran to the door. "MUM!" she bellowed down the hall. "Max has come downstairs. He's playing in the kitchen with a monkey."

"Quick, Toby," hissed Max. "You have to hide!" He looked frantically round the room. There was only one place he could think of. "Can you hold your breath?"

"Yes." Toby grinned. "For ages!" He closed his mouth and ducked under the bubbles just as Mum burst into the kitchen. Jessica peered slyly round her from the hall.

"What are you doing, Max?" demanded his mother. She looked very angry. "You were told to stay in your bedroom."

Agent Max had to put his super brain into gear and think fast. "I was . . ." he began. Then it came to him. "I felt so bad about the mess I made upstairs that I came down to do the washing up for you," he declared triumphantly, splashing his hands about in the water and pulling out a wooden spoon.

"Oh, Max," said his mum, her face softening. "That's so sweet. Thank you. We'll leave you to it." She turned to Jessica. "Come on, Jess," she said brightly. "Bedtime."

"But I want to see the monkey!" Jessica wailed.

"What monkey?" asked Mum.

"Max has got a monkey in the sink."

Max didn't know how long Toby could hold his breath. He had to get rid of Mum and Jessica quickly. More fast thinking was needed. He picked up the sponge and squeezed it so it looked like a mouth.

"Ooo-ooo, eee-eee!" he squeaked, making the sponge jiggle about. "This is what she thought was a monkey. I was just mucking about."

"**NOOOOO!**" yelled Jessica, stamping her foot. "He had a real monkey. It had ears and a tail."

Mum peered at the soapy suds. Then she grabbed Jessica and hauled her out of the door.

"Nice story, Jess," she said, "but you have to go to bed now."

They went, Jessica protesting all the way.

With a huge splutter, Toby burst out of the water.

"That was close," breathed Max. He looked at all the dirty plates. "But now we've got to do the washing up for real."

"Dangling drainpipes!" exclaimed Toby. "Can't wait. I love water and bubblz."

He stuck the sponge on his arrow-shaped tail, grabbed a plate in each front paw and scrubbed them clean.

"Awesome!" cried Max. "Two in one go. Wish I had a tail."

They soon had everything washed and piled in a wobbly tower on the draining board.

"Great work!" said Max, impressed.
"And we only broke a plate and three
glasses."

There was a noise from the hall. Toby
jumped into the breadbin as Dad came in.

"Good job, Max." He patted him on the
shoulder. "Go off and play now. I'll do the
drying up."

"Thanks, Dad,"
said Max. He
sidled round
towards where
Toby was hidden.
Somehow he had
to get him out of
the room without
Dad seeing. He
opened the breadbin a crack. There was
Toby, tucking into a large crusty loaf.

"You can't do that!" Max whispered.
"That's breakfast."

"Max, why are you talking to the

breadbin?" Dad asked, puzzled.

"I saw a mouse in there," said Max. He made a grab for Toby and stuffed him up his jumper. "It's OK. I've got it. I'll take it away."

He slipped out of the kitchen and dashed up to his bedroom, leaving Dad staring at the bread and the large, gargoyle-shaped teeth marks in it.

"Right!" Max said, shaking Toby out onto the bed and snatching up his Game Boy. "It's your turn now."

Toby gave a huge yawn. "Too tired," he said in a sleepy voice. "Bedtime."

He scrambled up into the wardrobe and made himself comfortable,

hanging upside-down from a coat hanger.
Soon Max could hear rumbling snores.

That'll keep him out of trouble, he thought
in relief, *until I get him back to school in the
morning. Then he can play all the tricks he
wants!*

4. Science and Snakes

Brrrrrrring! The bell rang for the end
of school. Everyone in Year Four jostled
out of Oldacre Primary and rushed home.
Everyone except Max and Ben. They were
mooching along the corridor to Science
Club.

"It's not fair!" moaned Max, dragging
his feet. "Why should Miss Bleet force us to
go to a stupid club after school? It's taking
up valuable gargoyle time. We haven't seen
Toby and his friends all day."

"It's not like we did anything wrong,"
agreed Ben. "We only put sherbet in Miss

Bleet's coffee to see what would happen. It bubbled up really nicely. I'd have thought that was enough science for one week."

Max opened the classroom door. His spy radar immediately picked up on someone in the front row: skinny, knobbly knees, ponytail. Max knew what that meant. It was Enemy Agent Lucinda Tellingly, codename: Bossy Boots. She was sitting smugly with her friend Tiffany. She stuck her tongue out at him. "I thought things couldn't get any worse," he muttered.

He and Ben sidled in to take their places at the back of the classroom and Max's spy radar whirred into action again: tall, bald, glasses on the end of his nose. It was Enemy Agent Mr Widget, codename: Boffin.

SPY FILE!

Codename:
Boffin

Mr Widget gulped as he saw them arrive. "Now we're all here at last," he said, rubbing his hands together nervously. "We're going to have such a good time!"

"I bet!" groaned Max under his breath.

"We are going outside to collect worms for a new wormery," Mr Widget continued.

Max let out a deafening whoop of joy and did a high-five with Ben. Maybe Science Club wouldn't be so bad after all.

"Glad you're so keen, boys." Mr Widget beamed, wiping his forehead with relief. "Now get into pairs, take one of these buckets of soapy water each – and follow me."

"Yuck!" came a disgusted muttering from Lucinda. "Why can't we pick flowers like we did last week?"

The Science Club kids marched out of school and over to the sports field, which was hidden behind a row of trees. They tried not to spill the contents of their red plastic buckets on the way.

"I wonder what this is for," said Max as he and Ben slopped along, leaving a trail of soapy water behind them. "Worms don't need washing, do they?"

Science Club arrived at the field. The far end was covered in sports equipment. The whole school had been practising for Sports Day. There were boxes of beanbags and balls, hoops and sacks.

Netting and long plastic tubes had been laid out for the obstacle course, there was a sandpit ready for the long jump, and in the far corner was a huge trampoline.

Mr Widget gathered the club around a patch of football pitch where the grass had been marked out in squares with string. "Our first task is to find out how many worms there are in the football pitch," he said.

"That's a silly idea, sir!" gasped Ben. "It'll take all night to dig them up."

"And then we won't be able to use the pitch for football," added Max, aghast.

"We won't be digging up the pitch," explained their teacher patiently. "We just pour the soapy water on these squares of ground and – hey presto! – the worms pop up. They always come up for soapy water. Then we count them and find the average number of worms in each square. We multiply that by the number of squares

that are marked out which gives us the number of worms in a quarter of the pitch, then we multiply that by four and – hey presto! – we find out how many worms there are in the whole pitch. Couldn't be simpler."

"Don't know what he's going on about," said Max, chucking some water on their patch. "Let's just find those worms!"

"Do we have to say *hey presto!* sir?" asked Ben.

"That will not be necessary," sighed Mr Widget. "When you have finished counting, you may each catch one worm and place it carefully in this pot of earth I've brought along. These will be the

worms for the new wormery."

All the kids in Science Club poured the water over their squares of grass and eagerly knelt down to wait. Max and Ben stared at their bubbly patch of earth. At first nothing happened. Then suddenly a little pink worm popped up behind a dandelion. There were squeals of horror from Lucinda and Tiffany as worms appeared on their patch of grass as well.

"Cool!" exclaimed Ben, watching all the worms wriggle to the surface. "It's working. Let's put some more water down and see if we can break the World Record for Worms in a Square." He turned to pick up the bucket, but it wasn't there.

"Someone's taken our water!" he declared indignantly.

The boys looked round. Max could just make out something red and plastic hidden in the hedge. "It's over there."

They hurried over. Sure enough, the bucket was hidden amongst the thickest leaves.

"How did it get in here?" Ben wondered.

"Afternoon," said a gurgly voice and a grumpy stone face appeared from behind the bucket.

"It's Bart!" cried Ben in delight as the round-bellied gargoyle waddled out.

"Have you come to join Science Club?" asked Max. "It's great. It's all about worms."

"Certainly not!" declared Bart grouchily. "Trying to get rid of Science Club."

Theo's cat-like head appeared from

the other side of the bucket. "We want
to get our pawz on the sports things,"
he explained, pointing a claw at the
equipment at the other end of the field.

"Been looking at it all day from the
church tower," grumbled Bart. "Thought
now school's finished we'd get our chance.
Then Science Club came out."

"I can't wait to play with the balls," said
Theo.

POP! Zack appeared out of thin air.
"Beanbagz and bats! Beanbagz and bats!"
he chanted, jumping up and down and
shaking the whole hedge.

"I wanted to explore those tubez" said a
shy voice.

Max peered deeper into the hedge. Barney was hiding there, the spikes on his back quivering with excitement.

"But why did you take our bucket?" asked Ben.

"If we collect all the buckets," said Bart, "Science Club won't be able to do any more science. Everyone will go away and leave us alone."

"Toby's doing it," added Barney. "It should have been Zack because he can make himself invisible but he kept reappearing by accident. He was nearly seen by the humanz."

There was a wheezy panting noise behind them and the boys turned to see Toby trying to haul a heavy bucket across the grass, water slopping everywhere. He wasn't getting very far. Suddenly he spotted the boys. He let go and flew back to the hedge.

"Greetingz." He grinned. "You're here just at the right time. I need you to collect all the buckets."

"It won't work," Max told him. "Everyone will just come looking for them like we did. You'll be keeping them here, not driving them away."

Toby scratched his stone chin. "Hmm," he said. "You may be right." He turned to his friends. "Listen, gargoylz, Trick One isn't working. We need Trick Two."

"What's Trick Two?" asked Max. "Can we help? Finding worms was fun but counting them will be boring."

"Max and Ben," came their teacher's voice. "What are you doing?"

Mr Widget was staring at them suspiciously.

"Er . . . some buckets rolled away, sir," called Ben. "We're just getting them back."

"Got to go," Max whispered to the gargoylz. "We don't want Mr Widget coming over here and finding you."

The boys grabbed the buckets and ran back to their square of ground. Suddenly a terrible stink filled the air and a wheezy laugh could be heard from the hedge.

"I think we've found out what Trick Two was." Ben grinned as the kids yelled in horror and dashed for the gate.

"Barney's made one of his special pongs! I hope the gargoylz have a good time on the sports stuff."

The boys held their noses and slowly walked after the rest of the fleeing Science Club. But the terrible smell didn't last long. Mr Widget headed the kids off at the gate and herded them all back to their task.

"Can't be put off by a silly little smell!" he exclaimed, picking up his pot. "Now start counting. And I'll come and collect your chosen worms."

"He's too busy to notice us for a moment," whispered Max. "And counting's boring. Let's go and find out if there's a Trick Three."

The two boys crept back to the hedge where the gargoylz were gathered in a circle, muttering to each other. Just then a stone head emerged from the leaves. It was a gargoyle that the boys hadn't seen before. It had plump cheeks and a wide grinning mouth, but instead of hair, stone snakes wriggled all round its head. The snakes writhed as if they were fighting.

"Wow!" breathed Max. "Who are you?"

"This is Eli," explained Toby. "Say hello to Max and Ben, Eli."

Eli looked horrified – and his snakes stood on end in shock. "Humansssssss!" he hissed.

"These are our friends," said Toby patiently. "They play tricks like us."

Eli's look of horror turned to a slow smile and the snakes on his head bobbed merrily at the boys.

"Eli is Trick Three," Toby went on. "He's going to use his special power to scare everyone off the field. Ready, Eli?"

To the boys' surprise, the snaky gargoyle suddenly vanished.

"Where's he gone?" asked Max, puzzled. "Can he make himself invisible like Zack?"

"Not exactly invisible . . ." said Toby mysteriously.

The next minute there was a yell from one of the kids counting worms.

"I've found a snake, sir!"

Toby grinned. "That's Eli," he said proudly. "He can turn into a snake."

They watched as Mr Widget rushed over to take a look, with the rest of Science Club following curiously behind him. Even Lucinda and Tiffany were edging cautiously forwards.

Toby gave a growly chuckle. "This is going to be more fun than the time I put earwigz in the vicar's wellies. Any minute now all those humanz will be screaming and running for their lives and we can have the sports things to ourselves!"

There was a muffled "Hurray!" from the hedge, and several pairs of eager stone eyes peeped through the leaves.

Mr Widget was now peering down at Eli. He still clutched his pot of worms. "A grass snake!" he exclaimed enthusiastically. "How interesting – and quite harmless. Look at its black spots and yellow collar." The children all jostled to look.

"No one's run away yet," commented Barney.

"I knew that idea wouldn't work," said Bart gloomily. "Kids aren't scared of snakes. At least not grass snakes, and that's all Eli can do."

"What about Trick Four?" asked Theo, swishing his tail.

"Haven't got a Trick Four," said Toby with a frown.

The gargoylz all looked despondent.

"I have!" exclaimed Max. "Lucinda and Tiffany are getting very twitchy about the worms and the snake has nearly finished them off. What if Zack makes himself invisible so no one will see him? Then he creeps up behind Mr Widget and knocks the worm pot out of his hand. Ben and I can make sure the worms land on Lucinda and Tiffany. People will hear their screams all the way to the moon!"

"Good one, Agent Black," said Ben. "Mr Widget will have to take them back to school and that will be the end of Science Club for today."

"Brilliant!" cried Zack, racing round in excited circles. Max noticed with relief that everyone in Science Club was still staring at Eli, so nobody spotted Zack. "Let's go!"

"Not yet, Zack," called Ben. "We've got to get everyone in position."

But it was too late. **POP!** Zack had vanished.

"Run!" Max told Ben urgently. "We've got to be there when the worms are spilled."

Max and Ben charged over to Mr Widget and stood just behind him, pretending to be keen to see the snake.

"He does look real," Max whispered as they watched Eli slither about the grass, his forked tongue darting in and out.

"Grass snakes should not be confused with adders," Mr Widget was telling his audience. "Adders are poisonous and— **Ooof!**"

He stumbled forward as if he had been given a hard push. Max caught a glimpse of Zack's dragony tail as it became visible for a second.

"Let me help you, sir," shouted Ben, making a grab for the pot. He gave it a quick upward jolt and the worms were flung in the air – falling all over Lucinda and Tiffany.

"Hurra— I mean, oh dear!" exclaimed Max, trying to hide his glee as the two terrified girls shrieked and jumped in shock, knocking buckets of soapy water over everyone's feet. Groans and complaints filled the air.

"I'm so sorry," said Ben, putting on his wide-eyed innocent look. "Let me help." Trying not to laugh, he started to pick worms out of Lucinda's hair. "Ooops! So sorry. That one went down your back."

"AAAARRRGGHH!" Lucinda screamed and sprinted for the gates, Tiffany close behind her.

"Wait!" blustered Mr Widget. "Or rather – yes, right, let's go in, everybody. Quickly now. All together. We'll collect worms another day."

Max and Ben followed the others out of the field, then Mr Widget locked the gates. Max and Ben peered back through the bars.

The gargoylz were having the time of their lives. Zack was darting about throwing beanbags to Theo, Barney's spikes were just disappearing down one of the tubes and Bart was playing in the sandpit. Eli was back to his normal self, bouncing on the trampoline, his snaky hair jiggling.

"Where's Toby?" whispered Max.

"Here I am," came a growly purr and

Toby flew up to perch on the gates. He was grinning broadly. "Thanks, Max and Ben," he said. "Now we're going to have the best gargoyle sports day ever!"

Gargoylz Fact File

Full name: Tobias the Third
Known as: Toby
Special Power: Flying
Likes: All kinds of pranks and mischief – especially playing jokes on the vicar
Dislikes: Mrs Hogsbottom, garden gnomes

Full name: Barnabas
Known as: Barney
Special Power: Making big stinks!
Likes: Cookiez
Dislikes: Being surprised by humanz

Full name: Eli
Special Power: Turning into a grass snake
Likes: Sssports Day, ssslithering
Dislikes: Birds of prey

Full name: Bartholomew

Known as: Bart

Special Power: Burping spiders

Likes: Being grumpy

Dislikes: Being told to cheer up

Full name: Theophilus

Known as: Theo

Special Power: Turning into a ferocious tiger (well, tabby kitten!)

Likes: Sunny spots and cosy places

Dislikes: Rain

Full name: Zackary

Known as: Zack

Special Power: Making himself invisible to humanz

Likes: Bouncing around, eating bramblz, thistlz, and anything with pricklz!

Dislikes: Keeping still

Collect them all!

1.

2.

3.

4.